First published in the United States 1989
by Chronicle Books
Copyright ©1986 by Naomi Kojima
All rights reserved
Printed in Japan
Type and jacket design by Karen Pike and
Julie Noyes
First published by Libro Port, Tokyo, Japan

Kojima, Naomi.
    The chef's hat / by Naomi Kojima.
        p.   cm.
    Summary: Andre, one of the finest
chefs in the country, is honored by the
Emperor's gift of a magnificently tall hat,
until he finds out how many problems
it causes in his life.

ISBN 0-87701-604-6
[1. Hats — Fiction. 2. Cooks — Fiction.]
I. Title.
P27.K83Ch 1989   88-30217
[Fic] — dc19   CIP
                                       AC

Distributed in Canada by Raincoast Books
112 East Third Avenue
Vancouver, B.C. V5T 1C8

10 9 8 7 6 5 4 3 2 1

Chronicle Books
275 Fifth Street
San Francisco, CA 94103

THE CHEF'S HAT

NAOMI KOJIMA

Chronicle Books • San Francisco

FOR KEI

Andre was the head chef at the Restaurant La Grande Pomme.

He was very young when he started to work
in the kitchen. Af first, he was given a small hat.
He peeled onions and washed potatoes. He
mopped the floor and scrubbed pots and pans.
But Andre dreamed of being a chef, and he
promised himself he would work hard until
he became one.

And Andre was the kind of person who kept
his word.

The years passed, and Andre's hard work and his love for cooking made him one of the finest chefs in the country. Now he wore the tallest hat in the kitchen.

One night, the Emperor, who was tired of the same old royal cooking, slipped out of the summer palace and went in disguise to the Restaurant La Grande Pomme.

The Emperor was so impressed by Andre's cooking that he summoned Andre to the palace the very next day.

There the Emperor awarded Andre with the tallest, most beautiful chef's hat in the country. Now, Andre had never wished for fame or prestige. The only thing that was important to him was cooking delicious food. Still, it was a grand honor. When the Emperor placed the shining, crisp, white hat on Andre's head, Andre was deeply moved.

"Your Majesty," Andre said in his quiet voice, "I shall cherish this hat and work even harder to deserve every inch of it. I shall take good care of it, and I will never, ever take it off."

And Andre was the kind of person who kept his word.

Andre was very happy. But when he got home,
he realized his promise wasn't going to be easy
to keep. He couldn't get through the doorway
with his hat on. So, being the kind of person
who keeps his word, Andre kept his hat on…

…and he and his family
celebrated under the stars.

That night,
Andre slept on the doorstep.

The next day, at the Restaurant La Grande Pomme, everyone was waiting to congratulate Andre. They all admired his beautiful, tall hat. But Andre had to keep his neck bent all the while, because his hat was higher than the kitchen ceiling.

By the end of the day, Andre had a terrible neckache.

With a bit of practice (and a lot of help from his family) Andre learned to get in and out of the house. But his life was no longer the same.

When he was inside, Andre couldn't stand up.
His hat was simply too tall. So all he ever saw
was the floor.

At the restaurant, the other chefs began to politely hint that Andre's hat was making it difficult for them to work.

And even everyday chores like laundry presented a problem.

His wife began to worry that the children would
forget what Andre looked like, since they never
saw his face anymore.

Andre was not happy.

Andre, who was once a hardworking, pleasant man, was turning into a sour person. Andre, who had the tallest chef's hat in the country, could not cook. His neck was stiff. His head hurt. He was tired all the time. But he had promised the Emperor that he would never, ever take his hat off.

And Andre was the kind of person who kept his word.

On his youngest daughter's birthday, Andre wanted to do something special. He decided to surprise his family by baking a cake. By twisting and bending, he managed to mix the batter, but, however hard he tried, he could not reach the oven.

"What's the use of such a hat when I can't even bake a simple cake?!" he cried. Then he threw the cake pan on the floor, kicked the kitchen table and burst into tears.

That night Andre made up his mind.

He went to the palace to see the Emperor.

Choosing his words carefully, Andre politely
described how his life with his hat had been.

"I can't stand up straight," he explained sadly. "And I can't cook. How can I be a chef if I can't cook? Please, Your Majesty," he said turning very red, "I just want to be an ordinary chef again. I'll do anything if you'll just take back your honorable hat!"

The Emperor was a bit surprised, but, being a resonable man, he could see Andre's point. After all, it *was* true. If Andre couldn't cook, he couldn't be a chef. And, since the Emperor loved good food, he wanted what was best for Andre and his cooking. So the Emperor took back the hat and shook Andre's hand.

"You're still the best chef, Andre, even without the hat," said the Emperor, looking at the dent Andre's hair had from wearing the hat for such a long time.

Andre rushed home from the palace. His head was light and so was his heart. He ran into the kitchen and made two yellow angel cakes with custard filling and pink icing. Then he woke his family and announced the good news.

They had a birthday celebration and toasted
Andre's courageous decision. Then, early the
next morning, the children delivered the second
cake to the palace.

A few days later, a large package arrived. It was a huge painting of a chef's hat. There was some writing at the bottom of the painting. It read:

For Andre,
because you are still the
best chef in the country.
   Love, Emperor
P.S. Thank you for the cake.
I ate it for breakfast.

With his family's help, Andre put up the painting in the dining room. It was very big and it covered much of the wall, but anything was better than a too tall hat.

For Andre

From then on, Andre was back to his happy self.

He worked even harder.
His cooking was better than ever.

And it is said that whenever the Emperor stayed at the summer palace, he often slipped out and went in disguise to the Restaurant La Grande Pomme. But no one ever knew for sure...because Andre was the kind of person who kept his word.